To Caroline, with love

First published in Great Britain in 1998
by Ragged Bears Limited,
Ragged Appleshaw, Andover, Hampshire SP11 9HX

Text copyright © 1998 by Elizabeth Dale
Illustration copyright © 1998 by Alan Marks

The right of Elizabeth Dale and Alan Marks to be
identified as the author and illustrator of this work has
been asserted

A CIP record of this book
is available from the British Library

ISBN 1 85714 145 8

Printed in Hong Kong

HOW LONG?

by Elizabeth Dale

illustrated by Alan Marks

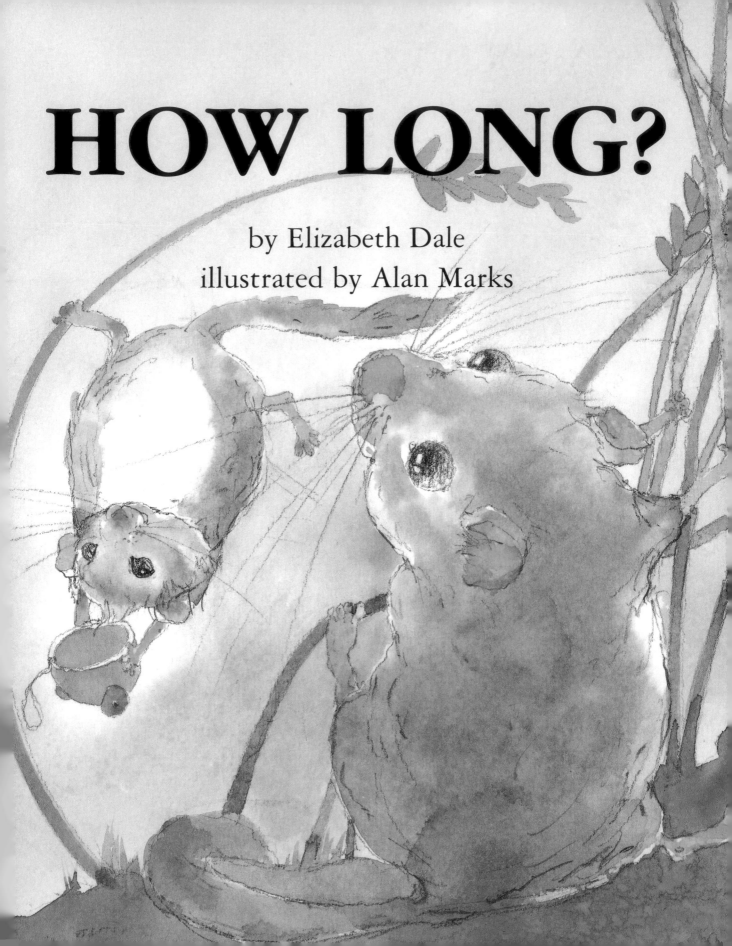

'Mummy?' asked Caroline.
'How long before you can
come and read me a story?'
'Oh, in a minute,'
said her mummy.

But how long was
a minute?

Caroline didn't know.
So she carried on painting
and painting.

'Here I am!' said her mummy.
Caroline looked at her painting.

That long!

'Mummy!' cried Caroline.
'How long until lunch?'
'Oh, about ten minutes,'
said her mummy.

But how long
was ten minutes?
Caroline didn't know.
So she lined up her trucks.

'Lunch is ready!'
called her mummy.
Caroline looked at her
long line of trucks.

That long!

'Mummy!' called Caroline.
'How long until you can play
with me?'
'Oh, about fifteen minutes,'
said her mummy.
But how long was fifteen minutes?
Caroline didn't know. So she
carried on digging in the sand.

'I'm ready now!'
called her mummy.

Caroline looked at her great
long tunnel.

That long!

'Mummy!' called Caroline. 'How long until the moon comes out?'

'Oh, about twenty minutes,' said her mummy.

But how long was twenty minutes?
Caroline didn't know.
So she carried on making her daisy chain.

'The moon is coming out now,' called mummy. Caroline looked at her daisy chain.

That long!

After tea, Caroline's mummy asked her to tidy up. 'You've got twenty minutes until bed-time!' she said. 'So don't be long!' Caroline smiled and looked at her daisy chain. Twenty minutes was a long time. So she started playing with her trucks... And her paints and her sand-pit...

And then, suddenly,
it was bed-time.

'Come on Caroline, I'll help you tidy up,' said her mummy. 'It's been a long day.'
Caroline looked at her painting, her trucks and her sand tunnel and her daisy chain.

'It has been a very long day!' she said, yawning.

She cuddled her mummy as they snuggled up in their nest.
'I do love you mummy,' said Caroline.
'I love you, too,' said her mummy.
'How long will you love me for?' asked Caroline.
'Oh,' said her mummy, as they looked up at the night sky.
'As long as it took to make all the stars in the sky and the moon and everything else there is.'

'That long!' said Caroline.
That was a very long time.
'And then will you stop
loving me?' she asked .

'Oh no,' her mummy replied.
'After all that long time,
I will only just have begun!'